W9-AJS-078

www.bigidea.com

www.zonderkidz.com

Sheerluck Holmes and the Hounds of Baker Street
Copyright © 2005 by Big Idea, Inc.
Illustrations copyright © 2005 by Big Idea, Inc.

Requests for information should be addressed to:
Zonderkidz, Grand Rapids, Michigan 49530

Library of Congress Cataloging-in-Publication Data
applied for

ISBN: 0-310-71150-9

Written by Doug Peterson
Editors: Amy DeVries and Karen Poth
Illustrations by Tod Carter
Art Direction: Karen Poth

Printed in China

05 06 07 08 • 7 6 5 4 3 2 1

Sheerluck Holmes and the Hounds of Baker Street

by Doug Peterson

Based on the VeggieTales® video
"Sheerluck Holmes and the Golden Ruler"

BIG IDEA BOOKS®

zonderkidz

Dogs howled
somewhere
on this foggy night
in London.

"Did you hear that?" asked Dr. Bob Watson.

"They say wild dogs roam Baker Street on nights like this," said Sheerluck Holmes, the world's greatest detective. "Perhaps this isn't a night to be out."

Suddenly, a policeman burst through the fog. Sheerluck gasped and accidentally breathed in on his bubble pipe.

"Come quickly!" shouted Scooter, the Scottish carrot constable. "Someone has disappeared at Doylie's Pizza Place!"

Sheerluck whispered to Watson, "I can't understand his accent."

"Did you say someone was speared by a dough boy with a pizza face?" asked Sheerluck.

"Ack!" Scooter motioned for the detectives to follow him.

They wound up at Doylie's Pizza Place.

"Sniffy disappeared right in the middle of a darts game," said a waitress. "Can you help us?"

"Certainly, my good woman. Where was Sniffy last seen?" asked Sheerluck.

"By the dartboard."

"Aha!" Sheerluck shouted. "I know what happened to Sniffy!"

"What is it?" asked Watson.

"His feelings were hurt and he ran away!"

"Wow," said the waitress. "Did you figure all that out by looking at clues like footprints and smudges on the wall?"

"No, I read this giant note," said Sheerluck. The note read: "You hurt my feelings! I'm leaving." Signed, Sniffy.

"The question is, who hurt Sniffy's feelings?" continued Sheerluck. "By the end of this night, I will know who that guilty person is!"

The game was afoot! Sheerluck moved through the room. He hunted for clues (and loose change) with his magnifying glass. He looked at each person one by one.

"Perhaps it was you, Morty Poppins!" he said. "You and Sniffy work together as chimney sweeps. Maybe you hurt his feelings."

"But...but..."

"Or maybe it was you!" Sheerluck said, whirling around. He stared at a plump guy named Nommy. "You always get mad at Sniffy for using big words. Maybe you hurt his feelings, Nommy."

For the next fifteen minutes, Sheerluck put on quite a show. Then came the moment of truth.

"I think I know who hurt Sniffy's feelings!" declared the great detective. "The culprit is none other than..."

Click!

The lights went out.

Tumble! Crash! Shout! Push!

After a few terrifying moments, the lights clicked back on. To Sheerluck's surprise, a crowd had tumbled into a big pile-up at the door.

"I'm to blame for turning out the lights," said Watson.

"You did? But why?" asked Sheerluck.

"Elementary, my dear Sheerluck! I knew the culprit would try to run under a cloak of darkness," explained Watson.

Sheerluck stared at all of the people piled up in the doorway. "But that means all of you hurt Sniffy's feelings. What kind of friends are you?"

"We're not very faithful friends," admitted Nommy. He looked very ashamed. "It's true. We all hurt Sniffy's feelings today."

Nommy explained, "Sniffy was competing in the All-London Darts Championship between Doylie's and Tower of London Fish and Chips. Doylie's could have won the game with one good toss of the dart. But right when Sniffy was about to throw, he sneezed. The dart missed by a mile. We lost the championship."

"We turned against Sniffy like a pack of wild dogs," confessed Morty Poppins.

"But faithful friends stick by each other even in bad times," said Sheerluck. "God says to treat others the way we'd like to be treated."

"How can we make it up to him?" asked Nommy.

"You can start by finding him," said Watson. "Look!"

Watson pointed to the floor. A trail of chimney soot led from the dartboard out the back door.

"Gadzooks!" shouted Sheerluck. "Judging by his trail, Sniffy ran out onto Baker Street!"

Baker Street. Where the wild dogs roam.

"We've got to save him!" shouted Nommy. "Who's with me?"

Everyone flew out the door and into the fog.

In the distance, they could hear dogs howling.

Were they too late? Was Sniffy doomed?

And then...

"He's over here!" shouted Morty.

It was almost too terrible to look. The dogs were all over Sniffy.

But wait!

"You're alive!" Nommy
shouted, overjoyed.

"These canine companions aren't
nearly as carnivorous as we presumed," said Sniffy.

"There you go with the big words again," said Nommy. "But
that's okay. The important thing is that you're safe."

"We're sorry we hurt your feelings," said Morty. "Can you ever forgive us?"

"Of course," said Sniffy. "You guys risked your lives to come look for me. You are faithful friends."

For the rest of the
night, everyone feasted on cake
at Doylie's—even the dogs. It was truly a special evening. They had learned
that faithful friends stick with each other in good times and in bad.

"A friend loves at all times.
He is there to help when trouble comes"

Proverbs 17:17